Tippy
and
Jellybean

The True Story of a Brave Koala
Who Saved her Baby from a Bushfire

Sophie Cunningham

illustrated by Anil Tortop

ALBERT STREET
BOOKS

Tippy and Jellybean live in a beautiful forest.
Their favourite trees are gum trees. Yum.

Their friends are possums, echidnas,
wallabies...and even the occasional *snake*.

Jellybean's best friend is a tree dragon.
His worst friends are the noisy cockatoos
that squawk right in his fluffy ears.

One day, Tippy and Jellybean wake up and
sniff the air. It's smoky, hot and windy.

Kangaroos and wallabies are bounding.
Wombats are scrambling to their burrows.
The cockatoos take off in an enormous flock.

Tippy can't hop. Or run. Or fly.

Her koala friends are climbing up to the very
tops of the trees, so Tippy starts climbing too.

When the noise gets really loud,
Tippy curls around Jellybean and closes her eyes.

Tippy is a *very brave mum.*

After the flames have passed, Tippy's fur
is singed and her paws are sore.

She touches Jellybean with her nose
to make sure he is okay.

There is nothing to eat and nothing to drink.
Tippy and Jellybean are very hungry.

A man finds them and encourages
Tippy to climb down the tree and
into his net. She holds Jellybean
against her tummy.

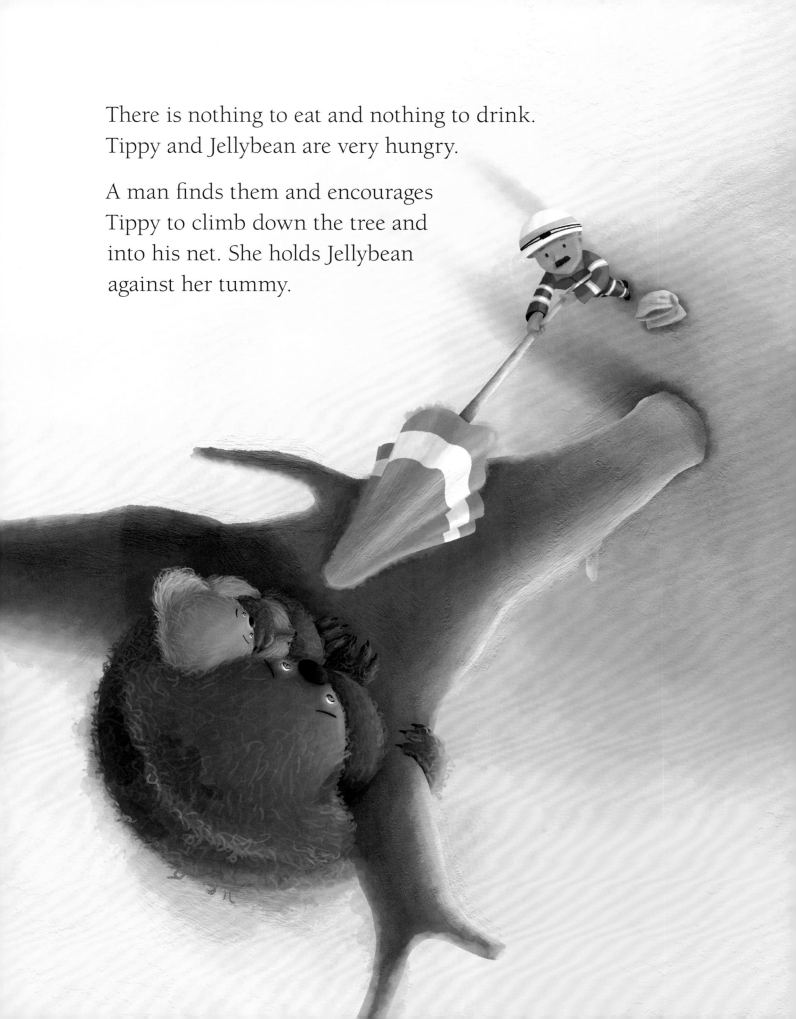

A long way away,
vets board a plane.
They are flying to help Tippy
and Jellybean and all their friends.

Kami is one of the vets.
She really loves koalas.

Tippy and Jellybean are waiting at the animal hospital. Nurse Evelyn has given them smoothies made from gum leaves and water, with extra vitamins.

'Right,' says Kami. 'Who have we got here?'

'This is Tippy,' Evelyn says. 'She protected Jellybean from the fires. That's why she has burns on her back.'

'You are very brave,' Kami says to Tippy.

Kami takes care of Tippy. Jellybean holds onto Tippy's tummy. He doesn't want to leave his mum.

Kami says that Tippy and Jellybean need lots
to eat and drink, and time to rest.

'Jellybean will stay close and keep his mum happy,'
says Evelyn. 'Those two are a team.'

Kami takes Tippy and Jellybean to an animal sanctuary where they can get better. They travel with their friends Gumnut, Spinach and Squeak.

Jellybean has never been this far from home.

At the sanctuary, Tippy and Jellybean sit in a tree that has been built just for them. They sleep a lot, and when they aren't sleeping, they munch on real gum leaves.

They munch

and MUNCH

AND MUNCH.

Soon, Tippy and Jellybean are
well enough to look after themselves.

'Time to get on with it, you two.'
Kami sounds practical, but she is
going to miss both of them *a lot*.

Tippy touches Jellybean with her nose.
They are home at last.

Six months later, there are lots of green leaves
on the trunks of the trees.

Jellybean is much bigger.
He can climb up to eat the bright
green leaves all on his own.

Yum.

The kangaroos come back, and so do the wallabies and the wombats. And those annoying cockatoos. The biggest, bossiest one sits on a branch and squawks in Jellybean's ear.

Jellybean just keeps munching.

He's a brave koala now, brave like his mum.

Photos by Marcia Riederer/DELwp

This book was inspired by the true story of Tippy and Jellybean,
two koalas from Gelantipy, East Gippsland.

$1 from every copy sold of this book will be donated to the
Bushfire Emergency Wildlife Fund, to aid the work of the vets who cared
for Tippy and Jellybean after their forest burned in the last days of 2019.

If you would like more information, please visit Zoos Victoria
www.zoo.org.au/fire-fund

Many koalas and other wild animals
were not as lucky as Tippy and Jellybean.
This book is dedicated to each and every one of them.